CAT NIGHTS

Jane Manning

GREENWILLOW BOOKS
An Imprint of HarperCollinsPublishers

elicity's goblin-green cake
blazed with candles.
It was her 263rd birthday.

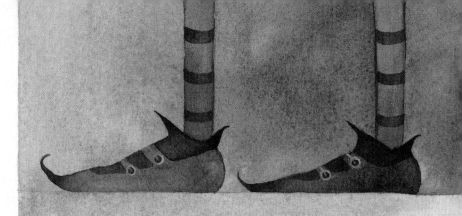

For a witch, 263 is a
very big year.
It's the year she grows
her first wart,

the year her shoes begin
to curl up at the toes,

and the year she's able
to cast her first love spell.

Felicity was as happy as a ghost on Halloween. But not because of the warts or the curly-toed shoes. She was happy because tonight she was finally old enough to turn herself into a cat.

Felicity couldn't imagine anything in the whole witchy world better than being a cat. "Please tell me about having whiskers and seeing in the dark! Is it fabulous?" she asked her older cousins.

"It's good, but flying on your broomstick is better!" Wanda said.

"I like brewing potions more," Willa added.

"Believe it. Brewing is best!" said Woo.

Felicity smiled a catty smile. Usually her cousins were right, she thought, but not this time.

Mugwort

Wolfbane

Dragon's Blood

The sun set and the moon rose. Felicity was so excited she could hardly say the words of the cat-changing spell.

"Give me whiskers and moonlight sight, as I become a cat tonight. My witchy self will now be gone, but I'll return by break of dawn!"

POOF!

Felicity's face sprouted whiskers and her fingernails became razor-sharp claws. She had night vision, and four-paw drive, and a beautiful long tail that switched and twitched for balance. With one sure leap, she was over the wall and gone into the night.

Felicity raced under the stars.

The moon looked so much *brighter* through a cat's eyes!

The wind seemed so much *fresher* through a cat's nose!

The earth moved so much *quicker* under a cat's paws!

The night seemed to pass in the blink of a cat's green eye.

But there are rules for just about everything in life, even for witches. Especially for witches.

For example:

Only a charmed broomstick can fly.

The fresher the newt, the better the spell.

And, a witch can change into a cat only eight times and still be able to turn back into a witch.

The ninth time, she
remains a cat for good.

However, rules were not on Felicity's mind the second night. She spent the whole day looking out the window, waiting for the sun to set over the trees, and planning what she would do once it did.

When the first stars sparkled in the
night sky, Felicity decided to find out
how fast she could run on her four
paws. She burst out the door, racing
across fields and farms and clear
through Briartown Woods.

On the third night, she joined some other cats to yowl at the moon.

On the fourth night, she used her strong tail for balance, leaping from roof to roof to roof all over town.

On the fifth night, she explored mysterious places, using her whiskers as her guide.

On the sixth night, she prowled about the Gellers' farmhouse, right under their sleeping noses.

By the seventh night, Felicity's cousins were certain
that she didn't care a whisker about the rules.
"Only two more nights," Wanda reminded Felicity.

"I know, I know!" said Felicity. Then she
leapt out of the window after a fat bat.

At the first hint of sunset on the eighth day, Felicity's
cousins sat her down and looked her hard in the eye.
"This is the last time, Felicity!" Wanda warned.
"The finish," said Willa.
"The enchanted end," said Woo.

Felicity saw that her cousins were worried about her.
She didn't want to upset them. After all, they'd taught
her how to fly on her broomstick and to cackle with style.
"Maybe I'll stay in tonight," Felicity offered.
"Good!" cheered Wanda.
"We can toast newts on the fire," said Willa.
"And make toadstool tea," said Woo.

But just as Felicity was about to toast her first newt, she felt the whisper of fresh night air coming through the window. It made her miss her whiskers and wish for her tail.

It was far too splendid a night *not* to be a cat!

In a flash, she was out the window, moonlight sparkling in her eyes.

Wanda, Willa, and Woo shook their heads and scratched their pointed chins. They knew they had no choice. For, as sure as brooms fly, at sunset tomorrow Felicity would change herself into a cat again.

Then no amount of magic could turn her back.

The next morning, while Felicity was sleeping, they whispered a spell over her.

"Cats are dusty, hairy, sneaky.

Smell like fish, scary, creepy.
Who would want to be a kitty?
Surely not Felicity."

The next evening Felicity slumped around the house, drank a glass of milk, and stared sadly out at the moon.

"Don't you want to be a cat?" Wanda asked, with a secret smile.

"Not tonight," said Felicity. She went to bed early.

Felicity hardly ate her dinner the next night.

"Would you like to take a spin on your broom?" Willa asked.

"Too tired," said Felicity.

The whole next day Felicity never even got out of bed.

"I think the spell we cast was a mistake," Wanda said.

"A bad idea," said Willa.

"A magical misstep," said Woo.

So, as Felicity slept, the witches whispered a spell remover over her.

"The spell we cast was a mistake.
It really was a boo-boo.
Remove our spell from Felicity,
so she doesn't feel
all boo-hoo."

Felicity woke up. It took only a moment for the sparkle to return to her eyes. She ran to the window and took a deep breath of cool night air.

"What a *beautiful* night to be a cat!" she cried.

"You know you've already changed eight times, Felicity," warned Wanda.

"This will be nine times," said Willa.

"Nine spells cast. This is your last," said Woo.

Felicity knew that it was the last time. She knew she could
never change back again. She knew she'd miss her cousins.
But she also knew one other thing: More than anything else
in the whole witchy world, she wanted to be a cat.

POOF!

And that's just what she became.

Note

The phrase "cat nights" comes from an old Irish legend. It says that a witch could turn herself into a cat eight times and still be able to return to her witchy self. But on the ninth time, she couldn't change back. From this legend comes the saying "A cat has nine lives." Since cats like to prowl about on summer evenings, especially in August, nights at that time of year have come to be known as "cat nights."

MEOW!

For Megan:
May you find your bliss
—with love, J. M.

Cat Nights. Copyright © 2008 by Jane Manning. All rights reserved. Manufactured in China. www.harpercollinschildrens.com. Watercolors were used to prepare the full-color art. The text type is 20-point Mramor Text. Library of Congress Cataloging-in-Publication Data. Manning, Jane K. Cat nights / by Jane Manning. p. cm. "Greenwillow Books." Summary: Felicity the witch begins turning herself into a cat as soon as she is old enough, and even though the rules say that she can only turn back into a witch eight times, she does it again on the ninth night. ISBN: 978-0-06-113888-1 (trade bdg.) ISBN: 978-0-06-113889-8 (lib. bdg.) [1. Witches—Fiction. 2. Cats—Fiction. 3. Identity—Fiction.] I. Title. PZ7.M31561Cat 2008 [E]—dc22 2007027685 First Edition 10 9 8 7 6 5 4 3 2 1

GREENWILLOW BOOKS